THE PRESIDENT OF THE JUNGLE

ANDRÉ RODRIGUES   LARISSA RIBEIRO   PAULA DESGUALDO   PEDRO MARKUN

Translated from the Portuguese by Lyn Miller-Lachmann

 Nancy Paulsen Books

NANCY PAULSEN BOOKS

an imprint of Penguin Random House LLC, New York

Visit us online at penguinrandomhouse.com

Library of Congress Cataloging-in-Publication Data is available upon request.

Manufactured in China by RR Donnelley Asia Printing Solutions Ltd.
ISBN 9781984814746
1   3   5   7   9   10   8   6   4   2

Design by Suki Boynton.
Text set in ITC Quorum Std.
The illustrations were made by mixing hundreds
of paper cutouts and loose pencil and charcoal doodles,
and then coloring them digitally.

37777124934514

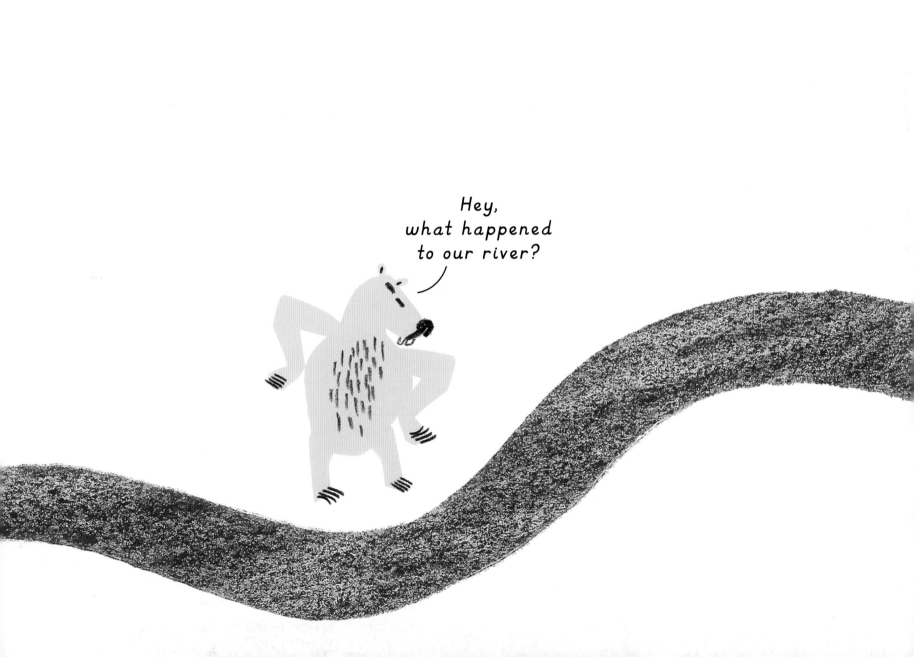

Lion wanted a swimming pool.
So, because he was King of the Jungle,
he rerouted the river to flow into his
front yard. Now he had his pool!

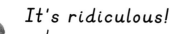

The other animals were not happy.
They missed their river. Lion had gone
too far! Maybe he should *not* be
King of the Jungle.

What if we had
a new leader?

Let's
protest!

We have
no water!
My children
are thirsty!

The animals decided to have a **demonstration**. They marched to Lion's swimming pool to protest.

But Lion couldn't care less what they thought.

So the animals decided it was time for a new leader.

In an election, anyone who wants to be the leader can become a **candidate** and put together a **campaign**.

Each animal gets to **vote** for the leader.

The candidate who gets the most votes becomes **president**.

Everyone liked the idea, so they drew up the rules for the election.

RULES
FOR THE
ELECTION

1) We will hold an election every spring.

2) Any animal can be a candidate.

3) Each animal gets one vote.

4) Votes are secret.

5) The candidate with the most votes wins.

6) Candidates cannot trade gifts for votes.

7) Candidates cannot eat their opponents.

Monkey, Sloth and Snake were excited
to become candidates.

CANDIDATES:
- Monkey
- Sloth
- Snake

Lion didn't want to be left out, so he became a candidate, too.

Then the campaigns began . . .

MY BELOVED SUBJECTS,

I descend from a long line of kings. It was my cherished great-great-grandfather who expelled the smelly possums so the rest of us could live in peace. I provided jobs to the animals who diverted the water from the river to build my swimming pool. If something is not broken, do not fix it.

For tradition, vote for Lion!

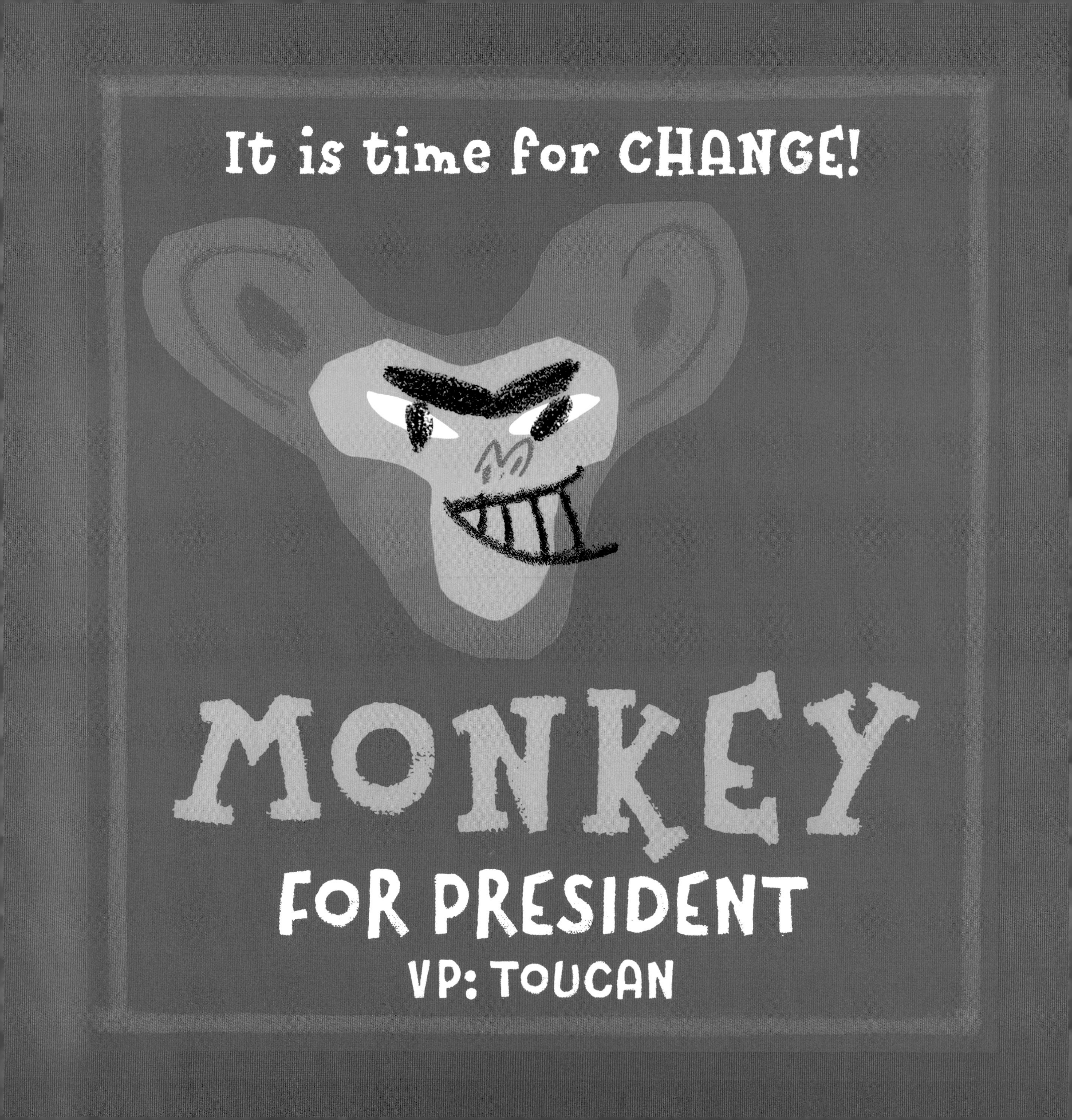
It is time for CHANGE!
MONKEY
FOR PRESIDENT
VP: TOUCAN

IT'S TIME FOR LION TO GO!

The king is sneaky and is as slippery as a rotten banana peel. He said we could all swim in his pool, and now we can't! Under my leadership, everything will be different. And we will build burrows and homes for everyone.

No more lies. Monkey for president!

SHE
DOESN'T
JUST
PROMISE...

SHE
DELIVERS!

SNAKE

FOR PRESIDENT · VP: MOUSE

I AM A POPULAR SNAKE!

I grew up in the jungle with all of you. I've crawled through burrows and nests getting to know you. We have faced the great drought together, and we have survived fires and hunters.

You know I will be there for you. Vote for Snake!

MAKE YOUR VOTE COUNT,

CHOOSE ME!

SLOTH
FOR PRESIDENT
VP: Ladybug

MY FELLOW ANIMALS,

It is time to plan our future together. I want to hear from all of you. And please don't judge me by my name. I am not lazy. I don't rush because good government does not happen overnight.

With patience, we will make the jungle better for everyone. Vote for Sloth!

Each candidate got busy trying to convince
the voters why they would be the best leader.

They went on TV,   took selfies with voters,

handed out pamphlets,   discussed the issues . . .

They held **rallies**.

Some said wild things
about the other candidates.

They put up posters   and discussed more issues . . .

They had **debates** to talk about their ideas.

EASY!
Every bird will
be assigned a
time to fly.

Why don't we
ask the birds
what they think?

Who cares?
Just tell those high-flyers
what to do!

Snake, how
would you
solve the bird
traffic jams?

Snake is venomous.

And sometimes they just argued.

Lion is selfish!

Well, nobody is better than me!

Hey! I didn't finish what I was saying . . .

Finally, Election Day arrived!
The animals lined up to cast their
secret votes in the **ballot box**.

Owl was in charge of counting the votes. Unfortunately, Lion got disqualified for violating rule number six. He had been giving voters peanuts so they'd choose him.

CANDIDATES

LION	SNAKE
MONKEY	SLOTH

When the votes were added up, the new president was announced. It was . . .

SLOTH!

The animals all gathered
to hear Sloth's victory speech.

"IN THIS ELECTION I LEARNED SO MUCH FROM EVERYBODY.

We each have something to say and we all should listen. Lion wants to be recognized for all his work. Monkey wants us to have food and shelter. Snake and I agree we are stronger when we work together. The first thing I will do as president is create a team to help us make the jungle a great place for *every* animal."

And that is the story of how Sloth
became the jungle's first president.

Of course, not everyone was happy with the election results. So it was a good thing that there would be another election next year!

A GLOSSARY OF ELECTION TERMS

BALLOT BOX: A box where the votes are collected. It can also be an electronic voting machine.

CAMPAIGN: The activities the candidate organizes to get elected.

CANDIDATE: A person or animal competing in an election.

DEBATE: A discussion among candidates where they present their ideas.

DEMOCRACY: The form of government in which the majority chooses its leaders through a vote.

DEMONSTRATION: A public meeting to express opposition or support for an issue.

ELECTION: The process of choosing a leader in a democracy.

GOVERNMENT: The group of individuals who lead, making the rules and the laws.

PRESIDENT: The top leader who governs in some democracies.

RALLY: A public gathering for candidates to drum up support for their ideas.

VP (VICE PRESIDENT): The leader who is second in command after the president, and who takes the place of the president if the president cannot govern.

VOTE: The process of making your choice in an election.

VOTER: One who votes in an election.